DEAD SEA OF ETIQUETTE

Nicholas Musteen

Dedication

To my wife Angela of 33 years (as of publication) and to her sister Amanda whose love of cruising inspires us all. And to the other Nicholas whom I loosely, only as inspiration, used as my character reference —the only people you kill is with your kind heart and personality. Keep on taking "Pictures with Strangers" my friend!

~Nic

First Edition – 2026

Paperback ISBN: 979-8-9950117-0-5
Published by: Nvisbl Media Group

CHAPTER Zero - Observations

Nick Smythe believed routine prevented error.

At forty-two, he no longer needed reminders. His habits ran automatically — wake at 5:45, black coffee, ten-minute stretch, news headlines skimmed but never absorbed. By 8:10 a.m., he was driving south toward Galveston, cruise ticket saved in his phone wallet, one medium suitcase secured upright in the back seat.

He cruised every ninety days.

Four sailings per year.

For fourteen years.

Even during the global shutdown of 2020, when ships sat silent in port and the world argued itself hoarse online, Nick had maintained the rhythm — not physically, but mentally. He had used that time productively. The absence of sailing created space for research. Deep research. Quiet research.

Pharmacokinetics. Enzymatic degradation. Time-to-symptom modeling. How certain compounds metabolized into indistinguishable cardiac events when introduced properly.

He had access others didn't.

Advanced EMT certifications opened doors.

Doors most people never thought to test.

Correction required patience.

And patience required discipline.

By 9:14 a.m., he stood inside the Galveston terminal, neutral expression, posture relaxed but alert. He wore jeans, a soft gray Henley, and boots scuffed just enough to suggest use but not neglect. He could blend anywhere — that had always been his advantage.

He scanned the room the way others might scan a buffet. Not hungrily. Just thoroughly.

Families clustered around luggage towers. Couples already irritated with one another. Diamond-status passengers drifting forward with subtle entitlement.

Observation preceded selection.

Always.

—

Across the terminal, Nic Stine adjusted his carry-on and scanned exits instinctively.

Fifty years old. Lean, deliberate. The kind of man who had learned to manage stress through metrics. His father had collapsed from a sudden cardiac event at fifty-three — no warning, no second chance. Since then, Nic had tracked everything. Sleep. Blood pressure. Market volatility. Patterns.

Especially patterns.

He wore a navy sport coat over a white button-down, dark jeans, and a well-worn pair of Lucchese cowboy boots. Not decorative boots. Broken-in leather, creased across the instep from years of actual use.

Beth stood beside him, her hand resting lightly on his forearm.

"You're mapping the room again," she said softly.

"I'm not mapping."

"You are."

Thirty years of marriage had taught her the difference between curiosity and over analysis. Beth didn't dull Nic's intellect — she steadied it. When he drifted into the weeds, she tugged him back gently.

"It's day one," she reminded him. "No spreadsheets."

He smiled faintly. "Right."

Behind them, Mandy Finley was filming the boarding process.

"Diamond boarding, baby," she whispered dramatically into her phone. "Know your perks."

Beth rolled her eyes with affection.

Mandy and Beth had been inseparable since childhood — nine months apart in age, close enough that life events had overlapped naturally. Weddings planned together. Babies born within months of each other. And now cruising.

Twelve times a year.

All Carnival.

Mandy treated loyalty like sport.

Johan stood beside her, hands in his pockets, quietly observant. At fifty-five, he still carried the calm detachment of a medical researcher accustomed to data sets and clinical trials. Early retirement circled his future, but he maintained every professional relationship carefully.

Patterns mattered in research.

He noticed things.

He noticed Nic scanning.

He noticed Beth steadying.

He noticed a man across the room watching without appearing to.

—

Nick's attention settled on the boots first.

Lucchese.

Real ones.

Heel worn slightly on the right edge — driver's side compression pattern.

Texas.

He stepped into the boarding queue as if by coincidence.

"Those real Luccheses?" he asked casually.

Nic glanced down, then up. "They've seen more airports than ranches lately."

Nick smiled faintly. "Forney?" he asked.

Nic paused. "Dallas."

"Close enough."

Nick extended his hand. "Nick. Forney."

"Nic. Dallas."

The name landed between them.

Mandy laughed immediately. "You've got to be kidding."

Beth smiled politely. Johan didn't.

Nick felt it — that subtle recalibration when two systems begin assessing one another.

"What do you do, Nic-from-Dallas?" Nick asked lightly.

"Data," Nic replied. "Mostly looking for what other people miss."

Nick's smile remained intact.

"I respect that."

And he did.

Assessment deserved respect.

—

Sail Away

By late afternoon, the Lido deck vibrated with pre-departure energy.

Music pulsed from overhead speakers. Crew members danced in choreographed enthusiasm. Plastic cups of frozen drinks multiplied quickly.

Mandy had already secured a table near the railing.

"Prime viewing," she announced. "You can't sail away from your cabin."

Beth leaned against the rail, ocean breeze lifting her hair.

Nic stood beside her, shoulders relaxing as the shoreline began drifting backward.

Balconies mattered to him because they created space. Perspective. The illusion of infinite room beyond narrow walls.

Nick appeared moments later with a beer in hand.

He blended easily into their circle.

"First night tradition?" he asked.

"Always," Mandy said. "You?"

"Every ninety days," he replied.

Johan's eyes lifted slightly at that.

“Religious about it?” Johan asked.

Nick smiled. “Routine keeps things balanced.”

Nic watched him carefully.

The ship’s horn sounded long and low.

People cheered.

Hands raised.

Music swelled.

Beth slipped her hand into Nic’s.

“Still feels good,” she murmured.

He nodded. “Yeah.”

Nick observed the group as the shoreline receded.

Mandy filmed again, narrating enthusiastically. Johan remained quiet but attentive. Beth leaned into Nic. The boots rested firmly planted against the deck.

Authentic.

Grounded.

Stable.

Nick respected stability.

But stability sometimes masked rigidity.

Rigidity, in confined ecosystems, created pressure.

And pressure demanded release.

He took a slow sip of beer.

“Here’s to smooth sailing,” he said.

They clinked plastic cups.

Nic met his eyes briefly.

“Smooth,” Nic echoed.

The word hung between them.

The ship turned toward open water.

Behind them, Galveston shrank into abstraction.

Ahead of them — seven days.

Seven contained days.

Nick felt the familiar sense of clarity settle in.

Correction did not begin on day one.

It began with observation.

And observation had just started.

CHAPTER ONE - Embarkation

Disorder doesn't begin at sea.
It boards with you.

Nick Smythe had stood at the Galveston terminal watching humanity misbehave before they had even crossed the gangway. The cruise hadn't started yet, but the fractures already had.

A man argued about boarding priority, voice rising just enough to make the staffer flinch. A woman stepped around the luggage queue as if the rules applied to everyone but her. Two teenagers shoved past an elderly couple without turning to apologize.

Nick didn't react.

He cataloged.

Confined spaces magnify behavior. Thousands of people sharing steel, air, and routine. The ecosystem only functions if cooperation outweighs entitlement.

Most people tolerate friction.

Nick did not.

He adjusted the cuff of his blazer and stepped forward when his group was called. Efficient. Polite. Unhurried.

“Morning,” he said to the terminal attendant.

She smiled instantly.

People always did.

Nick was built for trust—clean haircut, relaxed shoulders, easy eye contact. The kind of face you don’t remember until much later.

Behind him, a man in a navy polo shirt muttered loudly.

“This is ridiculous. It’s not that hard to run a line.”

Nick didn’t turn.

But he listened.

Tone reveals more than words.

The complaint wasn’t about delay. It was about status.

He filed it.

The atrium erupted with light and steel drums when he boarded. Staff clapped. Champagne trays floated through the crowd. Vacation energy pulsed thick and loud.

Nick integrated seamlessly.

"Pictures with Strangers?" he asked lightly, lifting his phone toward a group near the bar.

They laughed.

"Sure!"

Flash.

Another group.

Flash.

Integration builds invisibility. The more faces you stand beside, the less singular you appear.

He reviewed the images briefly. Everyone smiling. Everyone relaxed. Documentation without suspicion.

Across the bar, Navy Polo reappeared.

"Hey! Buddy! Two more beers!"

The bartender's shoulders tightened visibly.

Small disruptions ripple outward.

Nick watched carefully.

Repetition confirms pattern.

Navy Polo didn't say thank you when the drinks arrived. He didn't look at the server either. He pivoted toward a nearby couple and inserted himself into their conversation without invitation.

"You guys first cruise?" he asked.

They nodded.

"Hope you're ready for chaos," he laughed.

The couple smiled politely, but their posture shifted—tightened, slightly defensive.

Nick noted the shift.

Projection masked as humor.

Early indicators.

He did not rush assessment.

Certainty required discipline.

By sunset, the ship cleared the horizon. The coastline dissolved into haze. Open water surrounded them in every direction.

Nick stood on the upper jogging track and watched the ocean darken.

Ships are systems.

Engines calibrated. Rotations scheduled. Safety protocols layered.

Systems thrive on predictability.

Humans disrupt that.

Below deck, laughter rose again—sharp, intrusive.

Nick didn't need to look.

Navy Polo.

The volume was slightly higher now. Alcohol loosening boundaries that were already thin.

Nick rested his hands lightly on the rail.

Pattern requires repetition.

One data point is personality.

Two is habit.

Three is structure.

The night was young.

He would wait.

Timing matters.

He exhaled slowly as the last light disappeared beneath the horizon.

Vacation had begun.

CHAPTER TWO - Formal Night

By the third day, patterns revealed themselves.

Nick didn't search for Navy Polo.

The man announced his presence.

Breakfast buffet—complaint about coffee temperature.

"Is this even fresh?"

The server apologized. It was fresh.

Pool deck—commentary about "lazy staff" while snapping his fingers for another towel.

Elevator—refusal to step aside for a wheelchair because "we're all getting off on the same floor."

The wheelchair moment mattered.

The elderly woman said nothing. Her husband said nothing.

Most people said nothing.

Nick stood at the back of the elevator and watched Navy Polo stare at the floor while the chair's wheels caught briefly against the threshold.

Avoidance is admission.

Not of guilt.

Of character.

The doors opened. Navy Polo stepped out first without looking back.

Nick followed at measured pace.

Data accumulating.

Still not enough.

Certainty required repetition.

Formal night amplified everything.

Polished shoes. Tight ties. Champagne flowing freely.

People perform on formal night. They curate versions of themselves.

Entitlement often slips through the polish.

Nick took a seat near the promenade bar with a clear view of the dining entrance.

Navy Polo arrived late.

Volume first.

"Hope they saved the good table for us," he declared loudly, as if someone had challenged him.

The hostess smiled professionally and led him inside.

Nick followed at a distance.

Dinner confirmed it.

Navy Polo interrupted the server mid-description of the evening's special.

"It's not oaky. It's overprocessed."

The table laughed politely.

The server's smile faltered—barely perceptible, but real.

Navy Polo leaned back, satisfied.

Public correction.

Micro-dominance.

Projection disguised as expertise.

Nick felt the clarity sharpen.

Behavior repeated across environments.

Service staff. Guests. Shared space.

Escalation consistent.

Still, he waited.

Across the dining room, Nic Stine observed too.

Not Navy Polo.

Nick.

Nick felt it.

The weight of a second observer in the ecosystem.

Nic's eyes were analytical. Curious. Not hostile.

Yet.

Nick raised his glass slightly in acknowledgment.

A friendly gesture.

Nic hesitated, then returned the nod.

Observers recognize observers.

That would require monitoring.

Two variables now.

He adjusted accordingly.

Later that evening, the piano bar filled quickly.

Energy loose. Alcohol deeper.

The singer missed a note.

Navy Polo didn't let it pass.

"Wrong key!" he called out.

The singer forced a smile.

The crowd laughed nervously.

Navy Polo continued.

"You gotta own it, man!"

A few people shifted uncomfortably in their seats.

Nick watched carefully.

Service belittling. Public correction. Volume dominance. No self-awareness.

Repetition confirmed.

Navy Polo pivoted toward a couple seated beside him.

"You two from Texas?" he asked.

They nodded.

"Figures," he laughed. "Explains the boots."

The woman's smile thinned.

The man's jaw tightened.

Nick saw it.

Escalation from staff to guests.

The ecosystem destabilizing.

Certainty reached threshold.

He set his drink down.

Did not rush.

Timing matters more than intent.

Navy Polo raised his glass again.

"People are too soft," he declared loudly.

Then—

He stopped mid-sentence.

The glass tilted.

A flicker of confusion crossed his face.

His hand moved to his chest.

The stumble backward felt almost theatrical—except it wasn't.

The chair collapsed beneath him.

The room froze.

For half a second.

Then chaos erupted.

"Oh my God!"

"Is he choking?"

"Somebody call medical!"

Chairs scraped violently against the floor.

The singer backed away from the piano.

Nick was already kneeling.

Calm.

Controlled.

“Give him space,” he said evenly.

Authority doesn’t require volume.

The crowd obeyed.

He checked pulse. Airway. Rhythm.

The rhythm stuttered irregularly.

Then faltered.

Medical burst through seconds later.

Defibrillator deployed.

Commands layered over panic.

Shock.

Navy Polo’s body jerked once.

Then stillness.

Another shock.

Another command.

Nick stepped back as soon as medical took control.

Hands visible.

Expression appropriately grave.

Around him, guests cried openly.

Someone vomited near the bar.

The singer stood stunned against the wall.

A medic looked up.

Subtle.

Professional.

Final.

A sheet drawn gently over a face.

The piano bar did not move for a long moment.

Nick stood slowly.

Adjusted his jacket.

Exhaled once.

Not relief.

Completion.

Across the room, Nic Stine watched him.

Nick did not look shaken.

He did not look triumphant.

He looked… settled.

Their eyes met.

Half a second too long.

Then Nick looked away.

Staff began clearing glasses.

Music did not resume.

The ecosystem had absorbed the fracture.

Nick walked toward the exit calmly.

No rush.

No hesitation.

In the hallway, away from the noise, he paused briefly.

Order restored.

CHAPTER THREE - Port Day

Turks & Caicos didn't look real.

The water was too clear. The sand too white. The air too bright to hold what had happened the night before.

For a few hours, the ship felt imaginary again.

Nic rode along the shoreline on a chestnut horse, salt spray misting his legs. Mandy shrieked when her horse stepped deeper into the surf than expected. Mark tried to look athletic. Bella enjoyed watching him try more than his success.

Kevin and Kyle debated sunscreen application like it was a strategic disagreement.

Peter Macintosh held Ridley's hand while Dobby sprinted ahead chasing crabs like they had insulted him personally. Ivy rolled her eyes in long-suffering teenage patience.

Normalcy flooded back in waves.

Nic laughed harder than he expected to.

He needed it.

For the first time since the piano bar, the weight in his chest felt manageable.

Nick rode at the far end of the group.

Relaxed. Integrated.

He smiled easily when the guide cracked a joke about sunburns.

"Pictures with Strangers?" he asked lightly when they dismounted.

Flash.

Horses against turquoise water.

Flash.

Wind lifting hair and salt.

Nick reviewed the images briefly.

Everyone alive.

Everyone unaware.

He slipped the phone back into his pocket.

Back onboard, the day softened.

Showers. Aloe. Afternoon naps.

By dinner, the ship had resumed rhythm.

At 7:43 p.m., the promenade music cut cleanly.

A soft chime sounded overhead.

The captain's voice followed—measured, professional, controlled.

"Ladies and gentlemen, this is your captain speaking."

Conversations lowered but did not stop entirely.

"Earlier this evening, one of our guests experienced a medical emergency. Despite immediate response from our onboard medical team, the guest has passed away."

No name.

No description.

"Our thoughts are with the family. Out of respect, we ask that you allow them privacy during this time."

The announcement ended.

Music resumed after a delay that lasted just long enough to feel insufficient.

Nic stared at his glass.

That was it.

No moment of silence.

No acknowledgment of disruption.

Just continuation.

Around him, murmurs bloomed.

"That's terrible."

"Was it the loud guy?"

"Probably heart attack."

Reduction happens quickly.

Events compress into explanation.

Nick lowered his eyes respectfully for a brief second.

Hand resting lightly over his chest.

Then he resumed conversation with the couple beside him.

Appropriate. Balanced.

Nic watched him.

He didn't look shaken.

He didn't look relieved.

He looked… complete.

The word disturbed Nic.

Complete.

Dinner drifted into inevitable territory.

"What actually happens," Bella asked quietly, "when someone dies on a cruise?"

Kevin answered first.

"They don't just… bury them."

Kyle nodded. "Ships have refrigeration units."

"For emergencies," Peter added.

"Like a freezer?" Dobby asked, eyes wide.

"Yes," Peter said gently.

Nic felt something twist in his stomach.

Procedural.

Contained.

The ocean keeps moving.

Nick cut into his steak calmly.

"Ships are prepared for everything," he said.

His tone wasn't dark.

It was factual.

Prepared.

Nic looked at him.

"How often does it happen?"

Nick met his gaze briefly.

"More than people think."

The answer landed heavier than it should have.

"You sound certain," Nic said.

"I work emergency response," Nick replied lightly. "Perspective changes things."

The table quieted.

The conversation drifted elsewhere.

But Nic's mind did not.

Later that night, lying in the dark, he replayed the captain's voice.

Medical emergency. Guest has passed. Allow privacy.

The words felt engineered.

Compressed.

Across the ship, Nick stood alone on his balcony.

Wind pressed against him.

Below deck, laughter had returned.

The ecosystem stabilized quickly.

It always did.

He closed his eyes briefly.

Order restored…for now.

CHAPTER FOUR - Residuals

The morning after a death, the ship doesn't go quiet.
It goes thin.

The same music plays. The same announcements chirp. The same breakfast stations rotate trays like nothing broke. But beneath the surface there's a faint hesitation—like a crowd that learned a new rule and doesn't know how to say it out loud.

Nic felt it in the pauses.

He felt it in how people lowered their voices when they passed the piano bar.

He felt it in how strangers looked a fraction longer at anyone wearing a lanyard that suggested medical access.

They didn't speak about it directly.

They circled it.

At the coffee station, someone said, “Wild, right?” and someone else said, “So sad,” and the rest was swallowed by the sound of grinders and the clink of cups.

Nic stood with Beth near the pastry case pretending to browse.

“I can’t get that announcement out of my head,” Beth whispered.

“It was… sterile,” Mandy said from behind them, already holding two coffees like nothing on earth could interrupt her morning routine.

Johan, half-awake, nodded without lifting his eyes from his phone. “That’s how institutions survive events. They compress them.”

Nic’s jaw tightened slightly.

Compress them.

That was what it felt like.

Navy Polo had been compressed into “a guest.”

A person had become a procedural interruption.

And the ship was already moving on.

“Maybe that’s normal,” Beth said, but her tone didn’t believe it.

"Normal doesn't mean right," Nic replied.

He took his coffee and started back toward the corridor.

Beth followed.

The hallway was bright, carpeted, quiet. Vacation quiet.

They rounded a corner—

And nearly collided with Nick Smythe.

Too close.

Not just in distance.

In timing.

Nick stepped aside smoothly, as if he'd anticipated exactly how much space they would need. His smile arrived quickly—natural, easy, disarming.

"Sorry," Nick said.

"Not at all," Nic replied.

They stood for half a second longer than necessary.

Nick's eyes were calm. Friendly. Direct.

"You were watching closely last night," Nick said.

Nic felt his pulse tick upward.

He kept his face neutral. “Everyone was.”

Nick’s smile didn’t change.

“Not everyone watches the same way.”

Beth shifted beside Nic. A subtle step closer, protective without intending it.

“What does that mean?” Nic asked.

Nick’s voice stayed light, conversational. The kind of tone people trust.

“Some people look at surface. Some look for structure.”

Structure again.

The word was placed carefully, like a chess piece.

Nic held Nick’s gaze. “And you?”

Nick’s expression softened, as if amused.

“I work emergency response,” he said. “You start noticing patterns.”

The answer sounded normal.

The delivery did not.

Nick stepped aside fully, giving them the corridor.

"Enjoy the rest of your cruise."

He walked away unhurried, not looking back.

Nic watched him until he turned the next corner.

Beth exhaled once. "He's intense."

Nic didn't answer.

Because intense wasn't the right word.

Precise was.

Later, the ship tried to be itself again.

Trivia in the lounge.

Pool games that required forced enthusiasm.

Theaters advertising comedy shows as if laughter were simply a matter of scheduling.

Nic sat with Beth on a shaded deck chair while Mandy disappeared into a boutique claiming she "needed to see what kind of irrational prices they were charging for sunglasses."

Johan wandered off with a book, looking grateful to escape conversation.

Nic stared at the ocean and tried to allow it to erase the previous night.

It didn't.

He kept seeing Navy Polo's face in the moment before confusion replaced entitlement.

The glass tilting.

The suddenness.

The way the entire room had inhaled.

And the way Nick had already been kneeling—already issuing commands—already in control.

That part returned over and over.

Not that Nick helped.

That Nick seemed prepared.

There's a difference between responding and anticipating.

Nic told himself he was overthinking it.

He had a history of that.

His father had taught him that a single moment can rewrite the rest of your life. One breath, one stumble, one inexplicable change in rhythm—and suddenly you're in a conference room watching adults shout words you can't understand.

Trauma trains the brain to search.

It does not always train it to stop.

Nic rubbed his thumb along the rim of his plastic cup, feeling for texture as if it could anchor him.

Beth looked over. "You okay?"

"Yeah," he said automatically.

He wasn't sure if it was true.

Near midafternoon, Nic went for coffee again.

Not because he needed caffeine.

Because he needed routine.

The coffee station was quieter now. Guests came and went without conversation. The hum of the machine felt louder than it should.

Nic poured slowly.

He turned—

And Nick was there again.

Not abrupt.

Not stalking.

Just… present.

Like a man who belongs everywhere.

"You don't think it was natural," Nick said calmly.

Nic didn't blink. "I didn't say that."

"You didn't have to."

Nick's tone remained friendly, but the words were a push.

Nic forced himself not to react.

"You like observing people," Nic said.

"Yes."

"Why?"

Nick's answer came too quickly to be casual.

"Patterns matter."

Nic felt something cold settle under his ribs.

“And what do you do with them?” he asked.

Nick held his gaze a beat longer than normal conversation would allow.

“That depends.”

Silence stretched.

Around them, the ship continued performing normal.

A child laughed somewhere down the corridor.

A staff member wheeled a cart of pastries as if nothing had died.

Nick’s smile returned, lightening his face.

“Careful leaning too far over the railing,” he added easily, as if offering a general vacation safety tip.

Nic stared at him.

Nick walked away.

Not rushed.

Not defensive.

Just… done.

Nic stood holding his coffee, feeling absurdly like he'd been warned.

Beth approached from the side, carrying two muffins.

"Everything okay?" she asked.

Nic didn't answer immediately.

He watched Nick disappear into the crowd.

"Yeah," he said finally.

But his voice didn't believe him.

That evening, Mandy returned triumphant with a bag.

"Guess what," she announced. "We got invited into the Family Feud audition tomorrow."

Beth blinked. "What?"

Mandy grinned. "They needed one more group, and a staff member heard us joking about it at lunch. We just have to show up with five people."

Johan looked up. "We have four."

Mandy's grin widened. "We'll find someone."

Nic's stomach tightened without warning.

Vacation logic said: fun.

Pattern logic said: risk.

"What if we don't?" Nic asked.

Mandy waved him off. "It's a silly game."

It was.

But Nic's mind returned to Nick's words.

Patterns matter.

Some people look for structure.

Nic looked past his family to the crowd moving through the atrium.

Smiles. Drinks. Photos.

And somewhere inside that moving ecosystem, Nick Smythe blended perfectly.

Nic felt a quiet certainty settle into place.

Whatever had happened in the piano bar—

Nick had been more than a bystander.

And tomorrow, when they needed a fifth person, Nic had the strange, unavoidable sense that the ship would provide one.

CHAPTER FIVE - Family Feud

The audition room was brighter than it needed to be.

Studio lights hung overhead, humming faintly. A temporary backdrop displayed the cruise line's logo beside oversized letters spelling FAMILY FEUD in cheerful block font. Folding chairs lined the perimeter. A clipboard circulated like it carried something more important than trivia.

Mandy thrived immediately.

"Oh this is going to be fun," she said, clapping once like she'd been cast in a daytime show.

Beth laughed. Johan shook his head but smiled anyway. Nic stood slightly behind them, absorbing the room.

People perform differently when they believe they're being watched.

A middle-aged couple practiced high-fives. A group of college kids shouted mock answers across the room. A woman in a sequined dress kept adjusting her hair in the reflection of her phone.

The ecosystem was loud.

Nic felt the need to restore order instinctively.

“We need a fifth,” Johan reminded them quietly.

Mandy scanned the room. “We’ll grab someone.”

Nic turned—

And Nick Smythe stepped forward as if summoned by thought alone.

“I can fill in,” Nick said easily. “If you don’t mind.”

His tone was light. Friendly. Effortless.

Mandy beamed. “Perfect! See? The universe provides.”

Nick’s eyes flicked briefly to Nic.

A small acknowledgment.

Not dominance.

Not challenge.

Recognition.

Nic forced a polite smile. “Sure. Why not.”

Nick joined their group seamlessly. He placed himself not at the center—but not at the edge either. Precisely balanced.

The host—a cruise activities director with amplified enthusiasm—clapped his hands.

“Alright teams! We’re just looking for energy and chemistry. It’s all about fun!”

Energy was abundant.

Chemistry was not.

They lined up shoulder to shoulder under the lights.

The host read the first practice question.

“Name something people forget to pack on vacation!”

Hands shot up across the room.

“Phone charger!” someone yelled.

“Sunscreen!”

“Underwear!” a man shouted from the back.

Laughter rippled.

Nic leaned toward the host. “Statistically, the most forgotten item is medication,” he said casually. “There was a travel study in 2021—”

The host blinked.

The room quieted.

Nic realized he hadn’t meant to interrupt.

He had simply… corrected.

The host recovered quickly. “Right! Medication! Great answer!”

The crowd clapped politely.

Mandy shot Nic a playful look. “Show-off.”

Beth elbowed him lightly. “Let them have fun.”

Nic laughed it off. “Sorry.”

But Nick didn’t laugh.

Nick watched.

Public correction.

Control masked as helpfulness.

Escalation? No.

But a pattern?

Possibly.

The next question came quickly.

“Name something people argue about on vacation.”

“Money!” Mandy shouted.

“Where to eat!” Johan added.

“Directions,” Beth said.

Nick waited.

Nic stepped forward again.

“Time management,” he said. “Poor itinerary planning causes most travel friction.”

The host smiled tightly.

“Okay! Sure! Time management!”

Another polite ripple of applause.

Nick felt it now.

Not anger.

Confirmation.

Nic corrected publicly without hostility.

He believed himself helpful.

Unaware of the ripple.

The audition ended quickly.

The host scribbled notes.

"Great energy!" he announced. "We'll post selected teams tomorrow!"

The group dispersed into laughter and chatter.

Mandy spun toward Nic. "You're not writing a dissertation on a cruise."

Nic held up his hands. "Noted."

Nick stepped beside him.

"You seem tense," Nick said lightly.

"I'm not."

"You are."

The words were calm. Observational.

Nic met his gaze. “I just like accuracy.”

“Accuracy is valuable,” Nick agreed. “Delivery matters too.”

The sentence lingered.

Nic felt a subtle heat rise in his chest.

“You think I was rude?”

“I think,” Nick said gently, “that public correction can feel different than intended.”

The phrasing was careful.

Non-accusatory.

Precise.

Nic exhaled. “It wasn’t personal.”

“Intent rarely is,” Nick replied.

The words carried weight beyond trivia.

Mandy returned, sliding an arm through Beth’s. “Drinks. Now.”

The group moved toward the atrium bar.

Nick followed without hesitation.

They gathered around a small circular table.

Music drifted down from the upper deck.

Mandy recounted the audition dramatically. Johan exaggerated her competitiveness. Beth laughed more freely than she had all day.

Nic tried to let the energy reset him.

Nick stood at the edge of the table, relaxed, listening.

“You ever done this before?” Mandy asked him.

“Games?” Nick shrugged. “I observe more than I compete.”

Nic caught the phrasing.

Observe.

Always observe.

“Why?” Nic asked.

Nick smiled faintly.

“People reveal themselves when they’re trying to win.”

It was delivered like a harmless joke.

But Nic felt it land.

“You think people change when there’s a prize?” Beth asked.

“No,” Nick said softly. “They become clearer.”

The music swelled briefly.

Laughter erupted from another table.

Vacation noise filled the gaps.

Nic studied Nick’s expression.

Calm.

Unthreatening.

Not a flicker of aggression.

Which made the unease worse.

Mandy lifted her glass. “To winning tomorrow!”

They clinked.

Nick met Nic’s eyes over the rim of his drink.

There was no hostility there.

Just assessment.

Later, as the group dispersed for the evening, Nick lingered beside Nic in the corridor.

"You overanalyze," Nick said quietly.

Nic didn't deny it.

"It's how I work," he replied.

"Be careful," Nick said gently. "Sometimes the thing you're looking for isn't there."

Nic held his gaze.

"And sometimes it is."

For a moment, neither man moved.

The air between them tightened—not from aggression—but from recognition.

Nick stepped back first.

"See you at the game," he said lightly.

He walked away.

Unhurried.

Nic stood in the corridor alone for a long moment.

He told himself it was ridiculous.

It was a cruise.

A game show.

A random medical emergency.

Patterns matter.

The phrase returned uninvited.

Nic went back to his cabin feeling something he couldn't name yet.

It wasn't fear.

It was proximity.

And proximity changes everything.

CHAPTER SIX - The Event

It began with a hollow beat.

Not fast.

Wrong.

Nic felt it before he understood it.

They were midway through rehearsal for the game. The activities director had gathered the selected teams in a smaller lounge to run through timing and buzzer order. Mandy was already overly competitive. Johan was pretending not to be. Beth squeezed Nic's hand each time he answered too quickly.

Nick stood one place down the line.

Relaxed.

Watching.

The host asked another sample question.

“Name something people lose on vacation.”

“Luggage!” someone shouted.

“Patience!” Mandy added dramatically.

Nic felt it then.

A stutter beneath his ribs.

A thud that didn’t complete.

He blinked.

The lights above him felt sharper.

The air thinner.

Beth leaned toward him. “You okay?”

“Yeah,” he said automatically.

Another hollow beat.

Harder this time.

Like a skipped stair.

The room tilted slightly to the left.

Nick’s voice cut through calmly.

"Sit down."

Nic hadn't realized he'd swayed.

The floor rose faster than expected.

His knees buckled.

The buzzers clattered against the table as someone shouted.

"Is he fainting?"

The hollow beat exploded into chaos inside his chest.

Irregular. Violent. Wrong.

He tried to inhale and found the air fragmented.

Beth's voice blurred.

"Nic—"

And suddenly—

He was sixteen again.

Fluorescent lighting. Conference room carpet. His father mid-sentence, laughing about something inconsequential.

Then stopping.

Hand pressing to chest.

The coffee cup tipping.

A chair scraping violently against tile.

"Dad?"

Adults shouting words that sounded foreign.

Move him. Call someone. Clear space.

Nic frozen in the doorway.

The first time he understood that a body could betray itself without warning.

Back to the ship—

"Clear!"

The word detonated through his skull.

His body jerked once as if lightning had passed through him.

He tasted metal.

Smelled ozone.

Another flash—

His father on a stretcher.

Face gray.

Eyes closed.

A paramedic shaking his head once.

Back to present—

The ceiling above him swam in and out of focus.

Nick's face hovered briefly above him.

Calm.

Composed.

Not panicked.

"Stay with me," Nick said evenly.

The phrase felt almost rehearsed.

Nic tried to speak.

His jaw didn't cooperate.

The rhythm in his chest scrambled violently again.

Hands moved across him—staff, guests, medical team.

Someone pressed oxygen to his face.

“Pulse irregular—”

“Get him to medical—”

“Run a tox screen.”

The word cut clean through the noise.

Tox screen.

Why?

Why would that be necessary?

Another shock.

His body arched again.

Then darkness collapsed inward.

When awareness returned, it did so in fragments.

White ceiling.

Beeping.

The smell of antiseptic.

Beth’s hand gripping his.

“You’re stable,” she whispered.

Stable.

The word sounded fragile.

He tried to sit up.

The world swayed but held.

A doctor stepped into view.

Middle-aged. Controlled. Professional calm.

"You experienced a severe arrhythmic episode," the doctor said.

Nic swallowed. "Why?"

"We're still determining that."

"You said tox screen," Nic managed.

Beth turned sharply. "Tox?"

The doctor hesitated only slightly.

"We run expanded panels when rhythm destabilizes unexpectedly."

Unexpectedly.

Nic forced his voice steady.

"And?"

"There was a trace compound present," the doctor said carefully. "We're confirming specificity, but it does not belong in your system."

The room tightened.

"What kind of compound?" Beth asked.

"One typically restricted to emergency medical contexts."

Emergency.

Medical.

Nick's face surfaced in Nic's mind without invitation.

Calm.

Prepared.

Present.

"It could be cross-reactivity," the doctor added quickly. "We don't want to jump to conclusions."

Nic nodded slowly.

His father had died from a heart attack.

Natural.

Sudden.

Random.

For weeks before this cruise, Nic had wrestled with quiet fear that his own body might one day echo that same collapse.

Genetics are patient.

They wait.

But this—

This didn't feel inherited.

It felt introduced.

The thought scared him more than biology ever had.

Across the ship, Nick stood on his balcony at sunset.

He replayed the sequence.

Onset timing: correct.

Proximity: controlled.

Delivery: discreet.

Duration—

Shorter than expected.

Recovery occurred.

Variance.

That was the problem.

Variance disrupts certainty.

He flexed his fingers slowly.

A slight tremor passed through them.

That had never happened before.

He inhaled deeply.

Recalibrate.

No further action this sailing.

Contain exposure.

Distance restores clarity.

Below him, the ocean swallowed the horizon in shadow.

Nick closed his eyes briefly.

Structure had held.

But something unexpected had entered the equation.

And unexpected variables do not stabilize easily.

CHAPTER SEVEN - Anomaly

Nic did not sleep that night.

Not fully.

Machines hummed softly in the ship's medical ward. A steady electronic rhythm replaced the chaos that had torn through his chest hours earlier.

Beth dozed in a chair beside him, her hand still wrapped around his.

Every time Nic drifted, he felt the hollow beat again.

Wrong.

Interrupted.

Engineered.

At 6:12 a.m., the ship's doctor returned with a second physician and a tablet.

“We’ve stabilized your rhythm,” the doctor said. “You responded quickly.”

Responded.

As if it had been an argument.

“And the compound?” Nic asked.

The doctor glanced at the second physician before answering.

“We confirmed a trace of a cardiac-active agent. It’s highly regulated. Typically accessible only through specific emergency certifications.”

Beth’s hand tightened again.

“Emergency like… hospital?” she asked.

“More specialized than general hospital supply,” the doctor replied carefully.

“Fire department access?” Nic asked quietly.

The doctor paused.

“It’s used in certain advanced cardiac response training and field protocols, yes.”

The room felt smaller.

Nic did not look at Beth.

He didn't need to.

He could feel her mind moving beside him.

"It could be contamination," the doctor continued. "Cross-contact. Accidental exposure."

"How?" Nic asked.

The doctor didn't answer directly.

"We've notified corporate medical. You'll be cleared for discharge with monitoring."

Cleared.

Released back into the ecosystem.

As if the ship were simply resuming course.

Two decks above, Nick watched guests gather for breakfast.

He'd slept normally.

Which annoyed him.

Variance should disturb equilibrium.

It had.

But not enough to fracture him.

He replayed the dosage calculation in his head.

Measured.

Precise.

Tested in controlled environments during training.

It should have induced a complete arrest window long enough to resolve.

Instead—

Stabilization occurred.

Unexpected resistance.

He considered variables.

Body mass? Pre-existing medication? Genetic irregularity?

He did not know.

Ignorance is destabilizing.

He disliked ignorance.

His phone buzzed with a message from the activities director confirming Family Feud teams.

The Stine group remained listed.

Interesting.

Nic had not disembarked early.

Recovery implied resilience.

Resilience complicates closure.

Nick placed the phone face down.

No further engagement.

Distance now.

Disembark clean.

Reset from land.

By late morning, Nic was allowed to return to his cabin.

The hallway felt longer than before.

Guests moved around him carefully, whispering.

He saw pity in some faces.

Curiosity in others.

Nick stood near the atrium staircase speaking with a couple from Ohio.

Laughing.

Relaxed.

As if the night had not occurred.

Their eyes met briefly.

Nick's expression shifted only slightly—concerned, appropriate.

"How are you feeling?" he asked as Nic approached.

The question was public.

Safe.

"Better," Nic said.

Nick nodded once.

"Good. These things can come out of nowhere."

Out of nowhere.

Nic held his gaze.

"Sometimes," he said.

Nick's smile remained.

“Rest up.”

He stepped aside.

Unhurried.

Nic felt the proximity like static.

Beth leaned close. “That’s him.”

Nic didn’t respond immediately.

“Yes,” he said finally.

The disembarkation announcement came earlier than usual.

“Due to an onboard medical situation, we will begin staggered departure procedures.”

The phrasing again.

Compressed.

Neutral.

Guests lined up with luggage.

Murmurs filled the stairwells.

Nic stood between Beth and Johan.

Mandy was uncharacteristically quiet.

"Are we overthinking this?" Beth whispered.

Nic watched Nick several rows ahead.

Alone.

Perfect posture.

Hands steady.

"No," Nic said quietly.

He didn't know that yet.

But something inside him had shifted.

This wasn't trauma echoing his father's collapse.

This felt deliberate.

Nick exited the ship without looking back.

On the gangway, sunlight hit his face cleanly.

No hesitation.

No rush.

As he stepped onto the terminal floor, he felt the first true disruption of his internal equilibrium.

Not fear.

Awareness.

Something had resisted.

Something had survived.

And survival creates narrative.

He disliked narrative.

Narrative draws lines between events.

Lines connect dots.

Dots form patterns.

Nick adjusted his blazer and merged into the terminal crowd.

Containment now required patience.

Distance.

Silence.

Behind him, Nic stepped into the same sunlight.

But he did not feel relief.

He felt the beginning of something else.

A question that would not compress.

CHAPTER EIGHT - Follow-Up

They saw him the morning after he landed.

No waiting.

No denial.

Nic sat in his primary care physician's office less than twenty-four hours after stepping off the ship. The fluorescent lights hummed faintly. The walls were a muted blue meant to calm people who didn't want to be there.

Beth sat beside him, hands folded too tightly in her lap.

Bloodwork was drawn again. EKG repeated. Ship records transferred.

The nurse smiled reassuringly. "Probably stress," she said. "Travel can do strange things."

Nic nodded.

He wanted it to be stress.

He wanted it to be exhaustion. Electrolytes. Genetics.

He wanted it to be his father.

That thought startled him.

Because for days before the cruise, he had quietly wondered whether the same quiet fault line that had taken his father might one day split him open without warning.

If that were true, at least it would be familiar.

At least it would be inheritance.

Three days later, the phone rang.

The tone was measured.

“Nic, I need you to come in,” his doctor said.

Measured is worse than alarmed.

Measured means chosen words.

He returned alone this time.

Beth insisted on coming, but he needed to hear it first without her expression guiding his reaction.

The doctor closed the door behind her.

"We expanded your panels," she began carefully.

Nic waited.

"There's enzymatic evidence consistent with exposure to a regulated cardiac agent."

The words did not land all at once.

"Exposure," Nic repeated.

"Yes."

"Meaning accidental contamination?"

"We cannot confirm that," she said.

"What kind of agent?"

She slid a sheet of paper across the desk.

He didn't recognize the compound name, but he recognized the classification.

Restricted.

Advanced emergency response use only.

He looked up slowly.

"Who has access to this?"

"Highly trained emergency medical professionals," she said. "Certain paramedic and firefighter certifications."

The room seemed to contract around that single word.

Firefighter.

Nick's face surfaced uninvited.

Calm. Present. Controlled.

"How would it enter my system?" Nic asked.

"Ingested. Introduced. Possibly delivered in a beverage."

The memory snapped into place with surgical clarity.

Sparkling water with lime.

Nick standing too close.

Nick asking if he was tense.

Nick watching.

Nic felt something inside him split cleanly in two.

For weeks, he had wrestled with the fear that he was becoming his father.

That his heart had betrayed him.

That history was repeating.

But this—

This was not history.

This was proximity.

“You’re certain?” Nic asked quietly.

“As certain as lab work allows.”

The doctor leaned forward slightly.

“This compound is not available to the public.”

Not random.

Not inherited.

Not coincidence.

Introduced.

Nic nodded once.

Calm returned to his face.

Not because he felt calm.

Because he felt focused.

He left the office and sat in his car for several minutes without turning the engine on.

He replayed every interaction.

The piano bar.

The hallway.

The coffee station.

The phrase: Patterns matter.

His father had died because a body failed.

Nic had almost died because someone decided.

The difference was unbearable.

He pulled out his phone.

He did not call Beth first.

He did not call Mandy.

He did not call Johan.

He called the local police department.

"I may be wrong," Nic said when the officer answered.

"I hope I am."

He explained carefully.

Cruise death. Cardiac event. Restricted compound. Firefighter present on multiple sailings.

There was a pause on the other end.

“Sir, that’s a serious allegation.”

“I understand.”

“It could be coincidence.”

“It could.”

Another pause.

“We can document it.”

Document.

Contain.

Compress.

Nic hung up feeling unfinished.

He waited twelve hours.

Then he searched for the nearest federal field office number.

He did not exaggerate when he called.

He did not dramatize.

He listed data points.

Cruise itineraries. Presence overlap. Toxicology anomaly. Emergency certification.

Silence followed.

Longer this time.

"Send what you have," the voice said.

That was the first crack in dismissal.

Across the state, Nick stood in the bay of his fire station reviewing equipment logs.

Routine audits had begun.

Inventory reconciliation.

Chain-of-custody confirmations.

Small things.

Normal things.

Except the captain's tone had shifted.

"There are minor irregularities," the captain said.

"Explainable," Nick replied calmly.

He walked through them.

Log by log.

Signature by signature.

He remained composed.

He had not removed enough to trigger systemic alarm.

He had been disciplined.

Precise.

Still—

A thin line of awareness threaded through him.

Variance had occurred.

Variance creates inquiry.

Inquiry creates exposure.

That evening, he stood at his kitchen sink staring at his reflection in the dark window.

He replayed Deck Fourteen.

The hallway.

The sparkling water.

He had maintained control.

He always maintained control.

But Nic had survived.

And survival invites investigation.

Nick exhaled slowly.

Recalibrate.

Distance.

Silence.

Structure restores equilibrium.

Across town, Nic sat at his kitchen table with Beth.

He told her everything.

Every word the doctor had said.

Every phrase Nick had used.

Beth didn't interrupt.

When he finished, she asked only one question.

"Do you think he meant to?"

Nic didn't hesitate.

"Yes."

The word settled into the room like a verdict.

And neither of them tried to compress it.

CHAPTER NINE - Convergence

Agent Ramirez did not promise anything.
That was the first thing Nic noticed about him.

He didn't dismiss. He didn't validate. He listened.

They met in a federal building that smelled faintly of toner and old carpet. The conference room was neutral in every possible way. A legal pad sat between them.

"Walk me through it again," Ramirez said.

Nic did.

Not emotionally.

Structurally.

Cruise itinerary. Presence overlap. Nick's profession. Compound classification. His own exposure.

Ramirez didn't interrupt.

When Nic finished, the agent leaned back.

"It could be coincidence," Ramirez said evenly.

"It could," Nic replied.

"But if it isn't," Ramirez continued, "we're talking about something deliberate, mobile, and very patient."

Nic nodded once.

"That's what I'm afraid of."

Ramirez tapped his pen lightly against the legal pad.

"We'll review toxicology from recent cruise deaths tied to those sailings."

Recent.

Plural.

"Quietly," Ramirez added.

"Why quietly?" Nic asked.

"Because if you're right, he adjusts."

Adjusts.

The word made Nic's pulse tick upward.

"Have you spoken to anyone else from the cruise?" Ramirez asked.

"No."

"Do not," Ramirez said firmly. "Let us move first."

Nic agreed.

He left the building with no assurance.

But he also left with something else.

Movement.

Three days later, Ramirez called.

"We found something."

Nic sat down before asking.

"What?"

"A flagged trace compound in a prior cruise death two months ago. Dismissed as noncontributory at the time."

"Same agent?" Nic asked.

"Same class. Same restriction level."

Nic closed his eyes briefly.

Pattern.

"How many sailings?" he asked.

"Working on that."

"Is he on your radar now?"

There was a pause.

"Yes."

It wasn't an accusation yet.

But it was no longer coincidence.

Claire Calloway hadn't meant to become part of this.

Grief doesn't feel investigative at first.

It feels suspended.

Her husband had collapsed on the promenade deck during sunset cocktails. They had been arguing lightly about whether to book another cruise that winter.

He had laughed.

Then stopped.

Medical emergency.

Passed away.

The words had compressed him into a report.

But Claire had kept the paperwork.

All of it.

Including the toxicology report that listed a faint irregular compound reading.

“Probably contamination,” the cruise line had said.

She had nodded at the time.

Grief blurs suspicion.

When Ramirez contacted her, she almost declined the meeting.

Almost.

They met at a quiet café near the port.

Ramirez laid out photographs.

Sailing manifests.

Nick Smythe smiling beside strangers.

Claire leaned forward slowly.

"He was there," she whispered.

"Yes," Ramirez said.

"He helped," she added.

"Yes."

Claire's fingers tightened around the edge of the table.

"He told me something after," she said.

Ramirez looked up.

"He said sometimes removal restores balance."

The air in the café shifted.

"You remember that exactly?" Ramirez asked.

"Yes."

She swallowed.

"I thought it was strange. Who says that?"

Ramirez did not answer.

Claire reached into her bag.

"I kept something," she said.

She placed a small sealed envelope on the table.

“What is that?” Ramirez asked.

“A secondary sample request copy. I asked for confirmation testing before they finalized the report. I never sent it.”

Ramirez stared at the envelope.

“Why didn’t you?”

Claire looked out the window toward the water.

“Because I didn’t want to believe someone chose him.”

Chosen.

The word reframed everything.

Ramirez nodded slowly.

“We’ll test it.”

Claire looked back at him.

“If you’re right,” she said quietly, “he’s done this before.”

“Yes,” Ramirez said.

“And if he’s done it before…”

Claire didn’t finish the sentence.

She didn't need to.

Across town, Nick noticed the change before it became visible.

Equipment audits intensified.

Training inventory reviewed twice.

A quiet request for supply chain reconciliation.

No accusation.

Not yet.

But scrutiny had weight.

His captain called him into the office late in the shift.

"There are minor discrepancies in advanced cardiac response supplies," the captain said.

Nick didn't flinch.

"Explainable," he replied.

He walked through documentation calmly.

Transfers logged. Usage recorded. Training allocations signed.

He had never been sloppy.

But variance had occurred.

Variance creates paper trails.

Paper trails create questions.

The captain nodded slowly.

“Make sure everything reconciles.”

“It will,” Nick said.

He returned to the bay and stood for a long moment beside Engine 4.

He replayed Nic’s collapse.

Recovery was not part of the intended sequence.

Survival introduces narrative.

Narrative attracts institutions.

Institutions seek structure.

Nick inhaled slowly.

He had always believed he was correcting erosion.

Now erosion was circling him.

Across the state, Nic received another call.

"The preserved sample confirmed," Ramirez said.

"Confirmed what?"

"Same compound."

Nic felt the room tilt slightly.

"How many sailings now?" he asked.

"Four," Ramirez replied. "With overlapping presence."

"And?"

"We're preparing a warrant request."

"How long?"

"Soon."

Soon.

It wasn't immediate.

But it wasn't abstract either.

Nic ended the call and sat at the kitchen table staring at the wall.

Beth entered quietly.

He looked at her.

"It's real," he said.

She didn't ask how he knew.

She could see it in his face.

In another city, Nick stood alone on his balcony again.

Wind pressed against him.

He felt it now. Containment tightening.

He had miscalculated one variable.

Nic had survived.

And survival had spoken.

Nick closed his eyes briefly.

Correction had never frightened him.

Exposure did.

CHAPTER TEN - Return Voyage

Nic booked the cruise under his middle name.

Not because he believed Nick checked manifests personally.

But because he understood pattern.

And if Nick understood pattern too, then introducing one more variable might matter.

Four-day sailing. Galveston departure. Short window.

Compressed time means compressed opportunity.

Beth didn't argue.

She didn't like it.

But she didn't argue.

"If he's watching for you," she said quietly, "won't this confirm it?"

"Yes," Nic replied.

"That's the point."

Ramirez had not encouraged the idea.

He also had not forbidden it.

"If he believes he has control," Ramirez had said, "he will behave predictably."

"And if he doesn't?" Nic asked.

"Then we adapt."

Adapt.

Nic disliked that word.

It implied movement without certainty.

But certainty was no longer available.

Nick saw the booking alert two days before departure.

Not because he searched for it.

Because he had begun searching for everything.

Public passenger groups.

Social media.

Tagged cruise hashtags.

Nic Stine’s name surfaced in a closed Facebook sailing group.

Under a variation.

But recognizable.

Nick stared at the profile photo.

Alive.

Focused.

Returning.

Interesting.

He leaned back slowly.

Predators understand pursuit.

But few expect to be hunted.

Nick considered the variable.

Was Nic reckless?

Or strategic?

He did not feel fear.

He felt… curiosity.

The thought of rebalancing the ecosystem appealed to him.

But exposure risk had increased.

Variance requires discipline.

He almost decided not to board.

Almost.

Then another thought entered.

Absence confirms suspicion.

Presence controls narrative.

He completed his own booking within the hour.

He did not hesitate.

Embarkation day felt different.

Nic noticed it immediately.

Not because the terminal had changed.

Because he had.

He scanned faces now.

Measured posture.

Cataloged movement.

Beth walked beside him, steady but alert.

Mandy and Johan followed, quieter than usual.

“We’re really doing this,” Mandy muttered.

“Yes,” Nic replied.

Nick boarded two groups later.

He was not alone.

Claire Calloway walked beside him.

Composed.

Controlled.

Nic felt his pulse tighten.

Claire’s presence shifted the geometry.

Nick saw him instantly.

A small lift of the hand.

Friendly.

Unbothered.

Claire followed Nick's gaze.

"You know him?" she asked.

"Previous sailing," Nick replied easily.

He did not look threatened.

He looked amused.

That evening, the atrium felt smaller than before.

Short cruises compress relationships.

No time to drift.

Nick approached their table casually.

"Didn't expect to see you here," he said.

"Vacation," Nic replied evenly.

Nick's eyes flicked to Beth briefly.

"How's your heart?"

Mandy stiffened.

"Strong," Nic said.

"Good," Nick replied lightly. "Wouldn't want unfinished business."

The sentence was wrapped in silk.

Claire's eyes shifted between them.

"What does that mean?" she asked.

Nick smiled gently.

"Inside joke."

Nic didn't smile.

Claire didn't either.

Ramirez boarded at the first port stop.

Quietly.

Security coordinated without spectacle.

Two plainclothes agents joined the manifest as late additions.

Containment requires proximity.

Nick sensed it before he saw it.

A shift in the way security scanned the atrium.

An extra pair of eyes near the promenade.

Institutional posture has a rhythm.

He recognized it.

The ecosystem had begun observing him.

Interesting.

The hunter had entered structured territory.

Nick adjusted accordingly.

No selection this sailing.

No correction.

Observe only.

Reset perception.

Distance suspicion.

Across the deck, Nic felt it too.

Tension humming beneath conversation.

Claire lingered near the railing that evening.

She studied Nick differently now.

Not grieving.

Assessing.

Nick joined her.

"You look like you're solving something," he said.

"Am I wrong?" she asked quietly.

"About what?"

"About you."

Nick held her gaze.

"People look for villains when they need order," he said softly.

"That's not what I'm doing."

"What are you doing?"

"Looking for truth."

Nick's smile softened.

"Truth depends on perspective."

Claire did not respond.

Because for the first time, perspective felt like camouflage.

Later that night, a passenger collapsed near the pool bar.

Random.

Unrelated.

Nick froze half a beat too long.

Then moved.

Efficient. Professional.

But Nic saw it.

The hesitation.

Small.

Real.

Medical stabilized the man quickly.

Nonfatal arrhythmia.

Claire watched Nick's hands.

They were steady.

But his eyes were calculating.

"You paused," she said quietly later.

"I assessed," Nick replied.

"You always assess."

The sentence carried weight.

Nick felt it.

Micro-fracture.

He did not like being measured.

Across the ship, Ramirez received confirmation.

"Toxicology cross-match complete," the lab tech said over the phone.

"Same compound."

Ramirez closed his eyes briefly.

"Secure him at next port," he said.

The ecosystem was tightening.

And this time—Nick felt it.

CHAPTER ELEVEN - Deck Fourteen

Wind pressed hard against the upper deck railing.

Few passengers came this high after dark. The music from below drifted upward in faint fragments—laughter, a bass line, the mechanical churn of celebration.

Nick stood alone near the edge.

Open water in every direction.

He preferred height.

Height offers perspective.

Footsteps approached behind him.

Measured.

Not security.

Not staff.

Claire.

"You said you needed to explain," she said.

Her voice carried steadiness, but not comfort.

Nick did not turn immediately.

"I do," he replied.

He faced her slowly.

Up here, there were no curated smiles. No ambient distraction.

"You think I hurt him," Nick said.

"I think you were there," Claire answered.

"I'm always there."

"That's not what I meant."

Silence stretched between them.

The wind flattened Claire's hair against her cheek. She didn't brush it away.

"You told me something after my husband died," she said.

Nick's expression remained neutral.

"I say a lot of things."

"You said sometimes removal restores balance."

The words felt heavier now than they had in the café months earlier.

Nick inhaled slowly.

"One loud man can destabilize an entire room," he said quietly. "Small fractures spread."

"That's not a crime."

"No," Nick agreed. "It's erosion."

Claire felt the air thin.

"You don't get to decide that."

Nick's jaw tightened just slightly.

"Someone does," he said.

"Who?"

He looked past her briefly toward the horizon.

"The system rarely corrects itself."

The words hovered dangerously close to confession.

Claire stepped closer.

"Are you hearing yourself?"

Nick's voice lowered further.

"They weren't improving."

The sentence slipped.

A shift from abstract to personal.

Claire's breath caught.

"You mean him," she said.

Nick didn't respond.

Because naming creates liability.

But silence can function as admission.

Footsteps sounded again—heavier this time.

Nic.

Ramirez.

Two security officers.

Nick saw them.

For one second—

His pupils widened.

Not fear.

Calculation.

Exposure threshold reached.

Ramirez stopped several feet away.

“Evening,” he said calmly.

Nick’s posture reset instantly.

Controlled.

Professional.

“Agent,” Nick replied, as if greeting a colleague.

Claire stepped back slightly.

Ramirez glanced between them.

“Mr. Smythe, we need you to join us.”

“Regarding?” Nick asked evenly.

“A few questions.”

Nick's expression did not crack.

"I respond to emergencies," he said calmly. "I don't cause them."

Legal pivot.

Ramirez nodded once.

"We'll need you to repeat that statement in a controlled setting."

Nick's eyes flicked briefly to Nic.

Their gazes locked.

This was no longer subtle.

No longer philosophical.

It was structure versus structure.

Nick looked back at Ramirez.

"Of course," he said.

He placed both hands lightly on the railing before releasing it.

For a moment, Nic thought he might bolt.

He didn't.

Nick stepped forward willingly.

Security moved in quietly on either side.

Claire watched his face carefully.

"You meant it," she said softly.

Nick met her gaze.

"Meaning is interpretation."

Then he walked between the officers.

Calm.

Unrushed.

As if this were simply another procedural transition.

Inside the controlled conference room, the air conditioning hummed louder than necessary.

Ramirez sat opposite Nick.

Claire and Nic remained outside.

"Before we begin," Ramirez said, "I want to clarify something."

Nick folded his hands neatly on the table.

"Yes?"

"You said you don't cause emergencies."

"That's correct."

"Multiple toxicology matches suggest otherwise."

Nick's eyes did not waver.

"Correlation is not causation."

"You were present at each."

"I am present in many places."

Ramirez leaned forward slightly.

"Removal restores balance?"

Nick held his gaze.

"In tense environments, yes."

"That's not what I'm asking."

Nick's mouth curved faintly.

"You're asking if I killed someone."

"Yes."

Nick paused.

A long one.

Then:

“No.”

The word landed cleanly.

Measured.

Ramirez watched him carefully.

Nick did not fidget.

Did not blink rapidly.

Did not sweat.

Chilling composure.

Outside the room, Nic stood with his back against the wall.

Beth had joined them now, pale but steady.

“Is he cracking?” she whispered.

“No,” Nic said quietly.

“He won’t.”

Inside, Ramirez closed the file slowly.

“We’ll be speaking again,” he said.

“I assumed as much,” Nick replied.

As security escorted him back toward the stairwell, Nick passed Claire.

She searched his face for remorse.

For regret.

For fracture.

There was none.

Only recalibration.

For the first time, though—

Nic saw something new.

Not panic.

Not guilt.

But recognition.

Nick understood now.

The hunt had inverted.

And inversion changes strategy.

CHAPTER TWELVE - The Warrant

The knock came at 6:12 p.m.

Nick knew before he opened the door.

The cadence was wrong for neighbors.

Too measured. Too deliberate.

He turned off the faucet slowly, dried his hands on a folded towel, and walked to the entryway without rushing.

Through the frosted glass, he saw two silhouettes.

Structured posture.

Institutional stillness.

He opened the door.

Agent Ramirez stood there.

Two uniformed officers behind him.

“Mr. Smythe,” Ramirez said evenly, “we have a warrant.”

Nick stepped back immediately.

“Of course,” he replied.

No protest.

No confusion.

No raised voice.

“May I see it?” he asked calmly.

Ramirez handed him the document.

Nick scanned it with clinical detachment.

Toxicology correlation. Multiple sailings. Material access discrepancy. Intentional introduction of a restricted cardiac agent.

The language was precise.

He handed the warrant back.

“May I get my jacket?” he asked.

“You may,” Ramirez said.

Nick moved through his house deliberately.

Shoes aligned near the door.

Mail stacked neatly on the counter.

The kitchen spotless.

He took his navy blazer from the hook and slipped it on smoothly.

For a brief second, he paused at the hallway mirror.

He adjusted the collar.

Not vanity.

Presentation.

When he returned to the doorway, he extended his hands without being asked.

The cuffs clicked closed.

Cold.

Final.

Metal is not emotional.

It is structural.

A neighbor across the street stepped onto his porch, phone already raised.

Recognition spreads quickly.

Nick did not look at him.

He looked straight ahead.

Outside, the evening sky was fading toward orange.

He inhaled once.

Not deeply.

Just enough to mark transition.

The ride to the station was quiet.

Ramirez sat beside him.

Neither man spoke for several miles.

"You could have left," Ramirez said finally.

Nick turned slightly.

"Left implies guilt."

"It also implies survival."

Nick considered that.

"I survive by structure," he said.

Ramirez studied him.

"And what do you call what you did?"

Nick looked out the window.

"Correction."

Ramirez didn't respond.

Because argument invites philosophy.

And philosophy muddies evidence.

The booking room smelled faintly of disinfectant and fatigue.

Fingerprinting.

Photograph.

Name recorded.

"Occupation?" the officer asked.

"Firefighter," Nick replied.

The word felt altered now.

Reclassified.

He was placed in a holding cell alone.

Fluorescent lights hummed overhead.

Steel bench.

Cinderblock walls.

Containment.

Nick sat down carefully.

Hands resting on his knees.

He replayed the variables.

Nic had survived.

Claire had preserved.

Ramirez had correlated.

Exposure.

Exposure was the flaw.

Not correction.

He leaned back against the wall and closed his eyes briefly.

Not in regret.

In recalculation.

Across town, Nic stood in his kitchen staring at the news alert on his phone.

Texas Firefighter Arrested in Cruise Death Investigation.

Beth stood beside him.

Mandy and Johan arrived minutes later.

The room felt suspended.

“It’s real,” Mandy whispered.

Nic nodded slowly.

“Yes.”

He felt no triumph.

No relief.

Only gravity.

Because proving something deliberate does not resurrect what was lost.

And it does not erase the fact that someone chose.

Ramirez called an hour later.

“He’s in custody,” he said.

"Will he admit it?" Nic asked.

Ramirez exhaled quietly.

"Men like him don't frame it that way."

Nic understood.

In the holding cell, Nick opened his eyes again.

He flexed his fingers slowly.

Steady.

He had not panicked on Deck Fourteen.

He had not panicked at the door.

He would not panic now.

Systems function.

Even here.

The ocean continued sailing without him.

Guests continued boarding.

Disorder continued existing.

No one corrected it.

He rested his head lightly against the wall.

The flaw had been visibility.

And visibility is correctable.

CHAPTER THIRTEEN - Leak

The footage surfaced before the indictment did.
Grainy body cam.

Evening light fading across a quiet suburban street.

Nick Smythe walking down his front steps in handcuffs.

Head upright.

Expression calm.

The clip ran twelve seconds.

It ran on every network.

Texas Firefighter Arrested in Cruise Death Pattern.

Pattern.

The word ignited faster than the video.

By morning, his name trended nationally.

Vacation Vigilante? Cruise Ship Serial Killer? Medical Hero Turned Monster?

Cable panels assembled themselves with predictable urgency.

A former prosecutor. A behavioral analyst. A retired cruise security consultant.

On split screens, anchors spoke in controlled tones while a still image of Nick smiling beside strangers filled the right half of the frame.

Pictures with Strangers.

The caption changed everything.

What had once been harmless vacation documentation now felt curated.

Strategic.

Premeditated.

Nick saw none of it directly.

The holding cell did not offer cable access.

But the change reached him anyway.

In the way the booking officer avoided eye contact.

In the way the second shift guard stared slightly longer through the bars.

Recognition.

Recognition alters power.

He was no longer invisible.

He was narrative.

He disliked narrative.

Narrative removes control from the subject.

Claire watched the footage from her living room.

Her phone buzzed continuously.

Friends. Reporters. Former cruise acquaintances.

She muted the television and leaned back into the couch.

There he was.

Calm.

Almost composed enough to seem wronged.

That composure unsettled her more than rage would have.

If he had shouted, resisted, flinched—

It would have humanized him.

Instead, he looked prepared.

As if this were simply another procedure.

Her eyes moved to the coffee table.

The sealed envelope had been replaced by an official evidence receipt.

The preserved sample had confirmed what she had not wanted to believe.

Chosen.

Her husband had not been unlucky.

He had been assessed.

The distinction was unbearable.

Nic watched the same footage in silence.

Beth stood behind him with one hand resting lightly on his shoulder.

Mandy paced.

Johan stood near the window, arms folded.

“He looks normal,” Mandy said finally.

“That’s the point,” Nic replied.

News outlets began cycling through archived cruise photos.

Nick at the pool.

Nick at the bar.

Nick on the jogging track.

Always smiling.

Always beside someone else.

Always integrated.

The montage became accusation without words.

Integration now looked like infiltration.

Beth leaned closer.

“He doesn’t look like a monster.”

“No,” Nic said quietly.

“He looks necessary.”

The word slipped out before he could stop it.

Necessary.

It had lived inside Nick's tone from the beginning.

Now it lived on national television.

In the holding cell, Ramirez entered quietly.

"You're famous," he said.

Nick didn't smile.

"Fame is distortion," he replied.

Ramirez sat across from him.

"We're filing formal charges."

Nick nodded once.

"As expected."

"You understand the scope?"

"Yes."

"Multiple counts."

Nick folded his hands loosely.

"Alleged."

Ramirez studied him carefully.

"Do you feel anything?" he asked.

The question wasn't procedural.

It was human.

Nick considered it.

"I feel that systems overcorrect when threatened," he said.

"That's not what I meant."

Nick met his eyes.

"Then you should ask a different question."

Ramirez stood slowly.

He had interviewed men who wept.

Men who denied.

Men who blamed.

Nick did none of those things.

That made him more dangerous.

Or more disciplined.

He hadn't decided which.

By evening, the phrase began circulating online.

Removal restores balance.

A reporter had uncovered Claire's earlier statement.

The words spread rapidly.

Comment threads fractured into camps.

He's a psycho. He's cleaning up entitlement. He's sick. He's necessary.

Necessary again.

Nick leaned back against the concrete wall and closed his eyes.

The system had framed him as predator.

Some would frame him as vigilante.

Both were inaccurate.

He did not hunt randomly.

He corrected.

The ocean did not apologize for storms.

Why should structure apologize for enforcement?

A faint tremor passed through his hand.

It stopped quickly.

Exposure unsettled rhythm.

But rhythm can be recalibrated.

Outside the station, cameras waited.

Inside the cell, Nick sat still.

Composed.

Measured.

Watching the system construct a version of him that did not include intention.

And intention, he believed, mattered most.

CHAPTER FOURTEEN - Indictment

The courtroom filled before the judge entered.

Reporters occupied the back rows. Sketch artists angled for a clear line of sight. The air carried a low, anticipatory hum—the sound of a story waiting to harden into record.

Nick sat at the defense table in a navy suit.

Clean.

Composed.

Hands folded neatly in front of him.

He did not scan the room for sympathy.

He did not avoid the gallery either.

He simply sat.

Agent Ramirez stood along the wall, arms crossed loosely, eyes steady.

Claire sat three rows back.

Nic and Beth took seats on the opposite side of the aisle.

They did not look at each other at first.

The judge entered.

The room rose.

“Be seated.”

The prosecutor stood.

“The State will demonstrate a deliberate pattern of targeted cardiac events across multiple cruise itineraries.”

Targeted.

The word carried weight.

Slides illuminated the screen behind her.

Cruise routes traced in red lines across a digital map.

Dates aligned in vertical columns.

Photographs appeared next.

Nick smiling beside strangers.

Deck chairs. Bars. Shore excursions.

Pictures with Strangers.

The caption beneath the slide read: Presence at All Confirmed Incidents.

A low murmur moved through the courtroom.

The prosecutor advanced the slide.

Toxicology overlays appeared.

Compound traces highlighted in yellow across three separate reports.

"All consistent with a restricted cardiac agent accessible through advanced emergency certification," she said.

Nick did not shift.

His defense attorney leaned toward him briefly.

"Stay neutral," she whispered.

He had no intention of doing otherwise.

Claire was called first.

She walked to the stand with controlled steps.

"Did you interact with the defendant during your cruise?" the prosecutor asked.

"Yes."

"After your husband's death?"

"Yes."

"What did he say to you?"

Claire's voice did not shake.

"He said sometimes removal restores balance."

The words settled heavily across the room.

The prosecutor paused deliberately.

"How did that statement make you feel?"

"Unsettled," Claire replied. "Because my husband didn't need removal. He needed help."

Nick's eyes remained forward.

Not on her.

The prosecutor shifted.

"Did you preserve additional documentation?"

"Yes."

"And did subsequent testing confirm the presence of a restricted compound?"

"Yes."

The prosecutor nodded once.

"No further questions."

The defense rose.

"Mrs. Calloway," the attorney began smoothly, "is it possible that grief has shaped your interpretation of a phrase?"

Claire held her gaze.

"Grief sharpens things," she said quietly. "It doesn't invent them."

The defense paused.

"No further questions."

Claire stepped down.

She did not look at Nick.

Nic was called next.

He felt his pulse steady—not spike.

Steady.

He took the stand.

"You survived an onboard cardiac event?" the prosecutor asked.

"Yes."

"And later learned a restricted compound was present in your system?"

"Yes."

"Did you confront the defendant?"

"Yes."

"What did he say?"

Nic hesitated only slightly.

"He asked how my heart was. Said he wouldn't want unfinished business."

The room shifted again.

The prosecutor nodded.

"Did he ever deny harming you?"

"No."

The defense rose.

"Mr. Stine," she began, "you have a background in data analysis?"

"Yes."

"So you're inclined to look for patterns."

"Yes."

"Could you have connected unrelated events?"

Nic met her eyes.

"I wanted it to be unrelated."

Silence.

"Was it?"

"No."

The word carried no drama.

Only certainty.

The final slide returned to the photographs.

Pictures with Strangers.

Nick beside guests who would later collapse.

The prosecutor faced the jury.

"He positioned himself within proximity repeatedly. He had access. He had motive."

"Motive?" the defense objected.

"Belief in correction," the prosecutor replied.

The objection was overruled.

Nick leaned toward his attorney.

"They misunderstand structure," he whispered.

She did not respond.

Because she understood something else.

Juries do not convict on philosophy.

They convict on evidence.

The judge reviewed the charges formally.

Multiple counts.

Intentional introduction of a restricted substance.

Premeditated harm.

The room held its breath.

Nick stood when prompted.

“Mr. Smythe, how do you plead?”

He did not hesitate.

“Not guilty, Your Honor.”

Clear.

Steady.

The words did not tremble.

In the gallery, Beth exhaled softly.

Mandy closed her eyes briefly.

Ramirez watched Nick carefully.

No flinch.

No crack.

Just discipline.

The gavel struck.

Trial dates set.

Outside, cameras surged forward as Nick was escorted through a side exit.

Microphones extended.

“Why did you do it?”

“Do you feel remorse?”

Nick did not answer.

Inside the holding area, he sat down again.

Calm returned like muscle memory.

He had expected accusation.

He had prepared for spectacle.

He had not expected how easily the word killer would attach itself.

He had never used that word.

Removed.

Corrected.

Stabilized.

Language shapes perception.

Perception shapes verdict.

He closed his eyes briefly.

They were constructing a version of him that excluded intention.

He found that inaccurate.

And inaccuracies disturb him more than accusation ever could.

CHAPTER FIFTEEN - Not Guilty

Jail was structured.

That surprised him.

Wake. Count. Meal. Lights dimmed. Lights out.

Repetition steadies rhythm.

Nick adapted quickly.

He made his bed with exact corners each morning. He folded his uniformed intake clothes with deliberate symmetry. He noted the cadence of guard rotations and the timing of tray delivery.

Systems exist everywhere.

Even here.

The first week passed without incident.

Other inmates watched him with cautious curiosity. News traveled quickly inside concrete walls.

"You the cruise guy?" one man asked from the next bunk.

Nick met his eyes briefly.

"Yes."

"You kill those people?"

"No," Nick replied calmly.

The man studied him, then shrugged.

"Wild."

Wild was inaccurate.

Wild implies chaos.

Nick preferred precision.

In the quiet hours before lights out, doubt arrived differently than expected.

Not loud.

Not accusatory.

Curious.

He lay on the narrow mattress and replayed Navy Polo.

The voice. The entitlement. The disruption.

But now, separated from the environment, the memory shifted slightly.

Navy Polo had been loud.

Crude.

Erosive.

But deserving death?

The word intruded again.

Death.

Nick had never framed it that way.

He had framed it as correction.

Stabilization.

Intervention.

But here, stripped of ocean wind and ambient noise, the difference felt thinner.

He turned onto his side and closed his eyes.

The hollow beat of Nic's survival replayed in his mind.

Variance.

He had accounted for dosage.

For timing.

For proximity.

He had not accounted for resistance.

What if resistance was not anomaly?

What if it was warning?

The thought unsettled him.

Not morally.

Structurally.

If correction creates instability—

Is it correction?

The fluorescent lights flickered once before dimming.

Nick opened his eyes again.

The system had not overcorrected.

It had responded.

He adjusted his framing.

The flaw had not been correction.

The flaw had been visibility.

Visibility invites intervention.

Intervention creates exposure.

Exposure creates narrative.

Narrative becomes charge.

The logic restored him.

He inhaled slowly.

Order returned.

Across town, Nic sat in his home office staring at the same photographs now used in court.

Pictures with Strangers.

He enlarged one image.

Nick's arm around a couple who would later collapse.

He zoomed in further.

Nick's smile was genuine.

That disturbed him most.

No hatred.

No malice.

Just calm.

Beth entered quietly.

"You're doing it again," she said.

"Doing what?"

"Replaying it."

Nic nodded.

"He doesn't think he killed them," he said.

Beth sat across from him.

"What do you think he believes?"

Nic leaned back.

"I think he believes he was necessary."

The word felt heavier now.

Necessary implies burden.

Responsibility.

Duty.

That framing frightened Nic more than anger would have.

Anger burns out.

Conviction sustains.

Back in the cell, Nick sat upright on his bed.

The tremor returned briefly in his right hand.

Faint.

Almost imperceptible.

He pressed his palm flat against his thigh until it stopped.

He had never tremored before.

Exposure disrupts rhythm.

He would recalibrate.

He had always recalibrated.

A guard paused outside his cell.

"You good?" the guard asked.

"Yes," Nick replied.

"Don't seem like the others."

Nick considered that.

"I don't intend to be," he said.

The guard walked on.

Lights dimmed fully.

Nick lay back again.

For the first time since arrest, the doubt did not fully dissipate.

It did not accuse him.

It did not condemn him.

It simply remained.

A question without resolution.

He did not push it away.

He placed it carefully beside the rest of the data.

Questions refine systems.

They do not destroy them.

Not yet.

CHAPTER SIXTEEN - Reframing

Doubt rarely announces itself.

It seeps.

It lingers at the edges of thought and waits for fatigue.

Nick did not fear doubt.

He examined it.

He treated it as he would any anomaly in a system—identify, isolate, determine impact.

On the seventh night in custody, he lay awake replaying the question that had unsettled him.

But deserving death?

The phrasing bothered him.

Because he had never evaluated deserving.

Deserving implies morality.

He evaluated destabilization.

He rolled onto his back and stared at the ceiling.

Language matters.

The prosecution used killed.

The media used murdered.

Online commentary used monster.

All inaccurate.

Correction is not murder.

Stabilization is not cruelty.

Intervention is not violence.

He cataloged his rules again.

Behavior reveals character. Repetition confirms pattern. Certainty before action.

Had he acted without certainty?

No.

Each instance had met threshold.

Public erosion. Escalation. Disregard for others.

He had waited.

Observed.

Confirmed.

The doubt shifted slightly.

What if tolerance is strength?

The thought resurfaced.

He followed it.

Tolerance of disruption allows systems to absorb variance.

But what if variance compounds?

What if no one intervenes?

He imagined the piano bar escalating further.

The ripple spreading.

Humiliation normalizing.

Entitlement infecting space.

The ecosystem weakens.

He closed his eyes briefly.

No.

He had intervened before the fracture widened.

The flaw had not been intervention.

The flaw had been pattern visibility.

Too many sailings.

Too many overlaps.

Too much integration.

He had underestimated narrative formation.

That was strategic error.

Not moral failure.

The distinction steadied him.

The next morning, during legal consultation, his attorney laid out the state's approach.

"They're building psychological framing," she said. "Vigilante narrative."

"I'm not a vigilante," Nick replied calmly.

"I know that," she said. "But juries respond to emotion."

Nick considered that.

Emotion destabilizes logic.

He did not operate on emotion.

"They'll lean heavily on the phrase removal restores balance," she continued.

Nick nodded once.

"Taken out of context."

"What was the context?"

"Systems correction."

She studied him for a moment.

"Jurors don't think in systems."

That, he understood.

Humans prefer stories.

Stories require villains.

He had been recast.

He did not like being recast.

Across town, Nic received a call from Ramirez.

"Defense is pushing alternative explanation," Ramirez said.

"What explanation?"

"Coincidence. Contamination. Misinterpretation."

Nic exhaled slowly.

"They'll argue he's just present."

"He was present," Ramirez replied.

"That's the problem."

Nic stared at the wall after the call ended.

The case was moving into abstraction now.

Intent.

Philosophy.

Perception.

Beth entered quietly.

"He still thinks he's right, doesn't he?" she asked.

"Yes," Nic replied.

"How do you fight that?"

Nic didn't answer immediately.

"You don't fight belief," he said finally. "You fight evidence."

Back in his cell, Nick sat upright.

He pressed his palms together lightly.

The tremor did not return that day.

He reviewed every interaction with Nic.

The hallway.

The coffee station.

The warning about the railing.

He had probed too openly.

Language had slipped.

Correction requires silence.

He had drifted toward explanation.

Explanation invites scrutiny.

He would not make that error again.

Trial would focus on technical doubt.

Access control.

Chain-of-custody variance.

Reasonable uncertainty.

The system that accused him could also be leveraged.

Structure can be repurposed.

The doubt that had unsettled him the night before felt smaller now.

Contained.

Reclassified.

Not guilt.

Refinement.

He leaned back against the wall.

Calm returned.

Chillingly composed.

He was not confused about his role.

He had removed instability.

The world simply disagreed.

And disagreement does not invalidate necessity.

CHAPTER SEVENTEEN - Divide

The country divided faster than the court docket moved.

Talk shows ran polls.

Is He a Killer or a Vigilante?

Clips replayed endlessly—Nick walking calmly in handcuffs, Nick smiling beside strangers, Nick's face in profile during arraignment.

Comment threads fractured into camps.

He's sick. He's cleaning up entitled trash. He's evil. He's necessary.

Necessary again.

The word migrated from court transcript to headline.

Necessary Correction? Necessary Monster?

Nick read none of it directly.

But his attorney summarized public tone during one meeting.

"You've become symbolic," she said.

"Of what?" he asked.

"Depends who you ask."

He considered that.

Symbolism removes specificity.

Specificity had been his strength.

He did not operate in archetypes.

He operated in patterns.

The idea that strangers were debating him as philosophy rather than fact unsettled him slightly.

Not because they condemned him.

Because some defended him.

He had never intended to inspire replication.

Correction requires discipline.

Public imitation introduces chaos.

Chaos defeats purpose.

That thought lingered longer than expected.

Nic watched the divide unfold from his living room.

He didn't engage online.

He didn't respond to interviews.

But he read.

He saw the comments praising Nick.

Saw the threads describing him as "doing what the system won't."

The language felt familiar.

Removal restores balance.

The phrase had metastasized.

Beth sat beside him on the couch.

"You okay?" she asked.

"People want simple villains or simple heroes," Nic said.

"And he's neither?"

"He's convinced."

Conviction unsettles more than rage.

Rage burns out.

Conviction persists.

Nic turned off the television.

"He thinks he was necessary," he said quietly.

Beth didn't argue.

She didn't need to.

In jail, Nick received a stack of printed letters.

Fan mail.

The guard dropped them on the bench with mild amusement.

"You've got admirers," he said.

Nick waited until the guard walked away before opening the first envelope.

You're doing what nobody else has the courage to do.

Second letter.

The world needs more men like you.

Third.

Clean up the weak.

Nick folded the letters carefully and placed them face down.

He felt something unfamiliar then.

Not pride.

Concern.

Admiration without structure leads to escalation.

Escalation without discipline leads to error.

He had operated alone.

Controlled.

Measured.

He had never advocated ideology.

He had never recruited.

The narrative now forming around him was undisciplined.

Dangerous.

He did not like being catalyst.

He preferred being correction.

That distinction mattered.

During pre-trial hearings, the prosecution introduced additional toxicology matches.

A fourth cruise.

A fifth.

Each trace small.

Each dismissed originally as contamination.

But together—

Pattern.

The courtroom air felt heavier with each slide.

Nick did not flinch.

He did not argue visibly.

He absorbed.

His attorney leaned toward him.

"They're building inevitability."

"Inevitable is perspective," he replied.

“Juries like inevitability.”

Nick considered that.

If they believed his actions were inevitable—

They would call him serial.

He disliked that word.

Serial implies compulsion.

He had exercised choice.

Choice is controlled.

Compulsion is not.

He had never acted from compulsion.

He had waited.

Always waited.

That night in his cell, he lay awake longer than usual.

The tremor returned faintly.

He pressed his hand flat against the mattress.

Necessary.

The word resurfaced uninvited.

Had he been necessary?

Or had he been intolerant?

The distinction narrowed again.

He imagined the piano bar if he had not intervened.

Laughter continuing.

Small humiliations compounding.

Life moving forward.

He imagined Claire's husband alive.

Arguing about booking another cruise.

He imagined Nic walking off the ship unscathed.

The ecosystem continuing with its imperfections intact.

Was imperfection instability?

Or simply humanity?

The question lingered longer this time.

He did not push it away immediately.

He examined it.

Then slowly—

He reframed it.

Correction is not cruelty.

Correction prevents greater harm.

He had intervened before erosion became fracture.

The world was uncomfortable with intervention.

That did not invalidate its necessity.

The tremor stopped.

His breathing steadied.

He closed his eyes.

Calm returned.

Not defiance.

Conviction.

Across town, Nic received another call from Ramirez.

"Indictment finalized," Ramirez said.

"When?"

"Next week."

Nic nodded slowly.

"Do you think he'll ever admit it?"

Ramirez paused.

"No."

"Why?"

"Because in his mind," Ramirez said quietly, "he didn't commit murder."

Nic ended the call and stared out the window.

Necessary.

The word felt like a shadow that would not leave the case.

And shadows distort everything they touch.

CHAPTER EIGHTEEN - Escalation

The trial began with evidence.
It escalated with narrative.

By the third day, the courtroom had developed its own rhythm. Jurors leaned forward during toxicology testimony. Pens moved in near-unison when sailing dates were displayed side by side.

Pattern was no longer theoretical.

It was projected.

The prosecution built slowly.

Chain of custody logs. Access records from the fire department. Inventory discrepancies in advanced cardiac response supplies.

Each detail small.

Together—

Structure.

Nick sat upright through it all.

Hands folded.

Expression neutral.

His attorney whispered occasionally.

"Stay steady."

He was steady.

But something inside him felt… narrower.

As if the room had shrunk without moving.

The defense's strategy hinged on doubt.

Cross-contamination.

Medical complexity.

Coincidental presence.

"Mr. Smythe is a first responder," his attorney told the jury. "He shows up where emergencies happen. That does not make him the cause."

Nick approved of that framing.

Cause and presence are not synonymous.

The defense called an expert to testify about how rare cardiac agents can appear in trace amounts without deliberate administration.

Possibility.

The word hung in the air.

Possibility introduces uncertainty.

Uncertainty preserves freedom.

Nick listened carefully.

He did not need sympathy.

He needed reasonable doubt.

Then the prosecution played the Deck Fourteen security audio.

Wind distorted parts of it, but the phrase cut through clearly.

"…removal restores balance."

The jurors shifted visibly.

Nick felt something unfamiliar then.

Not fear.

Exposure.

Language had been his miscalculation.

He should have remained abstract.

Silence is discipline.

He had drifted toward explanation.

Explanation creates record.

His attorney stood quickly.

“Context matters,” she argued.

“Context is evident,” the prosecutor replied.

The judge allowed it.

Nick kept his breathing steady.

Inhale four.

Hold.

Exhale.

He had trained his body to remain controlled under fire.

This was not different.

Except—

He could not command this room.

He could not reposition this narrative.

He could only endure it.

Claire testified again during rebuttal.

She described the moment on Deck Fourteen.

“He wasn’t angry,” she said.

“He wasn’t grieving. He was… convinced.”

The word hung heavily.

Convinced.

Not unstable.

Not impulsive.

Intentional.

Nic watched from the gallery.

He could see it too now.

Nick was not unraveling.

He was defending a philosophy.

That made the case heavier.

Because philosophy resists evidence.

During a recess, Nick stood in the holding corridor outside the courtroom.

His attorney spoke quickly.

"They're leaning hard on intent."

"I can see that," he replied calmly.

"You need to look human."

"I am human."

"That's not what I mean."

He studied her.

"Do you want me to cry?"

She didn't answer.

Because juries equate emotion with remorse.

Remorse softens.

Conviction hardens.

Nick did not know how to soften something he did not frame as wrong.

The tremor returned briefly in his right hand.

Stronger this time.

He clasped his hands together until it stopped.

For one second—

A thin slice of panic surfaced.

What if the system is right?

The thought was sharp.

Intrusive.

He closed his eyes.

Breathed.

Systems respond to disruption.

He had disrupted.

The system was responding.

That did not prove moral failure.

It proved friction.

The panic receded.

Reclassified.

Not guilt.

Physiological stress.

Understandable.

Containable.

Closing arguments arrived faster than expected.

The prosecutor stood before the jury with no slides this time.

"No manifesto," she said. "No rage. No chaos. Just calm correction. That's what makes this dangerous."

Nick did not react.

"You don't need anger to commit harm," she continued. "You need belief."

Belief.

The word echoed.

The defense rose.

"Belief is not murder," she countered. "Presence is not guilt. Possibility is not proof."

Nick watched the jury carefully.

Some avoided his eyes.

Some studied him directly.

One juror—a middle-aged man with wire-rimmed glasses—held his gaze longer than the rest.

Not hostile.

Curious.

Nick held it.

Steady.

Chillingly composed.

He would not give them fracture.

He would not give them spectacle.

If they convicted him, it would not be because he collapsed.

It would be because they rejected his structure.

And rejection does not negate necessity.

When the jury retired to deliberate, the courtroom emptied slowly.

Nick remained seated.

Hands folded.

Calm restored.

But deeper now—

The doubt had not disappeared.

It had only quieted.

Waiting.

CHAPTER NINETEEN - Verdict

The jury returned in less than six hours.

Nick noted that.

Not too fast.

Not too slow.

Deliberation time signals narrative alignment.

He stood when instructed.

The courtroom rose with him.

Claire sat rigid.

Nic's hands were clasped so tightly his knuckles had blanched white.

Beth leaned into him slightly.

The foreperson stood.

"On the charge of intentional introduction of a restricted cardiac agent resulting in death…"

The pause expanded the room.

"…we find the defendant guilty."

The word did not detonate.

It settled.

Heavy.

Inevitable.

Nick did not flinch.

Did not blink.

Did not exhale audibly.

The judge continued reading counts.

Guilty.

Guilty.

Guilty.

Each one layering structure around him.

The courtroom noise began only after the final count.

A muffled wave of breath.

Someone sobbed softly.

Claire did not.

She stared forward.

Nic closed his eyes briefly.

Relief did not arrive the way he expected.

It felt quieter.

Less triumphant.

More final.

Nick remained upright.

Hands folded.

He turned his head slightly toward the jury.

Not accusation.

Assessment.

They had chosen order.

Just not his version of it.

Sentencing came two weeks later.

The courtroom felt smaller.

Less crowded.

The spectacle had moved on.

The judge reviewed aggravating factors.

Premeditation. Pattern. Abuse of professional access.

Nick listened without visible reaction.

"Life imprisonment without the possibility of parole," the judge concluded.

The gavel struck.

Sound carries differently when it finalizes something.

Nick allowed himself one slow inhale.

The ocean returned in memory.

Deck Fourteen.

Wind pressing hard.

Black water endless beneath steel railing.

The ecosystem humming below.

He had believed himself guardian.

Corrector.

Necessary.

The word returned with full clarity now.

Necessary.

Was he?

The tremor did not return.

The doubt did not surge.

He examined the question one final time.

If left unchecked, would erosion spread?

Yes.

If intervened upon, would systems resist?

Yes.

Had he miscalculated visibility?

Yes.

Was intervention wrong?

Silence followed the question.

He did not answer it emotionally.

He answered it structurally.

The system had rejected him.

Systems reject disruption even when disruption exposes fragility.

He had been the friction.

The system had absorbed and neutralized him.

That did not invalidate the imbalance he had seen.

It only invalidated his method.

He stood when instructed.

Turned.

Allowed the bailiff to secure him.

Cold metal again.

Final.

As he was led from the courtroom, he passed Claire.

Their eyes met.There was no rage there.

No triumph.

Only distance.

He passed Nic next.

Nic held his gaze.

For a brief second, neither man moved.

Structure versus structure.

Correction versus containment.

Nick inclined his head almost imperceptibly.

Not apology.

Acknowledgment.

Then he was guided through the side door.

Out of view.

In the transport vehicle, steel grate separating front from back, Nick rested his head lightly against the window.

The city blurred past.

People walking sidewalks.

Traffic lights cycling.

Order maintained imperfectly.

He closed his eyes.

The ocean remained vivid in memory.

Black water. Steel railing. Wind.

He replayed his final thought on Deck Fourteen months earlier.

Removal restores balance.

The world had interpreted it as confession.

He interpreted it as principle.

He did not feel monstrous.

He did not feel righteous.

He felt resolved.

In the quiet hum of the vehicle, with chains resting loosely against his wrists, he spoke softly to no one.

"I was necessary."

There was no hesitation. Outside, the world continued.

Imperfect.

Uncorrected.

And indifferent to his conviction.

CHAPTER TWENTY - Aftermath

Prison had rhythm.

Count. Meal. Silence. Movement. Lock.

Nick adapted within a week.

Maximum security was louder than county had been. Harder. Less controlled. The ecosystem here did not pretend to be orderly.

Men shouted down tiers. Arguments sparked over nothing. Televisions blared conflicting realities.

Instability everywhere.

Nick observed.

He did not intervene.

He did not advise.

He did not recruit.

That mattered.

He kept to himself, read case law from the prison library, and ran structured physical routines in the narrow space beside his bunk.

Three inmates approached him during the first month.

“Cruise guy, right?”

He nodded once.

“You were cleaning up people.”

“I was correcting imbalance,” Nick replied calmly.

The man laughed. “That’s one way to say it.”

Nick did not elaborate.

He disliked how loosely they held the concept.

Correction requires precision.

Their tone suggested chaos.

He withdrew further.

Isolation preserves clarity.

Outside, the narrative shifted again.

Books were announced.

Streaming rights rumored.

Podcasts dissected timelines and toxicology.

Nick Smythe became a case study.

Psychology panels debated vigilantism.

Law schools examined intent versus pattern.

He listened when news filtered through other inmates.

He did not react.

Symbolism had overtaken specificity.

He was no longer a man.

He was thesis.

Claire refused interviews.

Nic declined media requests.

Beth ignored documentary producers who called twice a week.

But Mandy—

Mandy read everything.

She watched one panel discussion and turned the television off halfway through.

"They're romanticizing him," she said.

Nic sat across from her quietly.

"They need a narrative," he replied.

"He doesn't get to be a narrative."

"No," Nic agreed. "He doesn't."

But narratives persist without permission.

Ramirez visited the prison once.

Not required.

Not formal.

Just a quiet closure.

They sat across from each other in a glass-partitioned room.

"You still believe you were correcting something," Ramirez said.

Nick met his gaze.

"Yes."

"You regret nothing?"

Nick paused.

"I regret miscalculation."

"Of dosage?"

"Of visibility."

Ramirez studied him carefully.

"No moral reconsideration?"

Nick considered the question longer this time.

"There is moral discomfort," he said finally.

Ramirez leaned forward slightly.

"That's something."

"It is not guilt," Nick added.

Ramirez nodded slowly.

He stood to leave.

"You know others will try to imitate you."

Nick's eyes sharpened.

"They won't succeed."

"You sound certain."

"They lack discipline."

Ramirez watched him for a long moment.

That was the first answer that unsettled him.

In the months that followed, two cruise ships reported unexplained cardiac events.

Unrelated.

Nonfatal.

But enough to stir headlines.

Copycat?

Speculation ignited instantly.

Nick heard about it through inmate chatter before the newspapers confirmed it.

He sat very still when he read the article.

He had not acted.

He could not act.

Which meant someone else had.

Correction without precision.

Intervention without structure.

That disturbed him deeply.

He folded the newspaper slowly.

Imitation is instability.

Instability spreads.

For the first time since conviction—

He felt something close to alarm.

CHAPTER TWENTY-ONE - Contagion

Nic read the same headline at 5:42 a.m.

Unexplained Cardiac Episodes on Cruise Ship Raise Questions.

He didn't need to read further.

He knew what the subtext would be.

Beth walked into the kitchen.

"You saw it."

"Yes."

"Do you think it's him?"

Nic shook his head.

"He can't."

"Then what?"

Nic stared at the paper.

Narratives propagate behavior.

He had studied this for years in business environments.

Market reactions. Consumer psychology.

People imitate perceived authority.

Even if that authority is distorted.

"He's become permission," Nic said quietly.

Beth understood immediately.

Permission to correct.

Permission to intervene.

Permission to judge.

The danger was no longer Nick alone.

It was the idea of him.

Ramirez called before noon.

"We're looking into it," he said.

"Copycat?" Nic asked.

"Possibly."

"Does he know?"

"We haven't told him."

Nic exhaled slowly.

"You should."

"Why?"

"Because if anyone understands what's wrong with it, it's him."

Ramirez considered that.

"He might enjoy it."

"No," Nic said. "He won't."

In prison, the news reached Nick two days later.

Two episodes. No fatalities. Investigation ongoing.

He read the article twice.

The dosages were imprecise.

Delivery inconsistent.

The victims random.

No pattern threshold confirmed.

This was not correction.

This was chaos.

He folded the paper carefully.

For the first time since incarceration—

He felt displaced.

Someone else had attempted structure without discipline.

And people would attribute it to him.

His attorney visited the following week.

"Public chatter is shifting again," she said. "They're calling it your shadow."

Nick's jaw tightened slightly.

"It is not."

"You don't control that."

He looked up at her calmly.

"I never intended to create a movement."

“Intent doesn’t matter anymore.”

That statement lingered long after she left.

Intent doesn’t matter.

That had been the prosecution’s thesis too.

He sat on the edge of his bunk that evening and replayed the phrase removal restores balance.

Had he made it too simple? Too transferable?

Correction requires criteria.

Criteria require discipline.

Discipline cannot be crowdsourced.

The thought unsettled him more than conviction ever had.

He had not wanted imitation…He had wanted containment.

CHAPTER TWENTY-TWO - Necessary

Winter arrived without announcement.

The prison yard grew colder.

Nick walked its perimeter in measured laps.

Breath steady.

Steps counted.

He replayed the copycat reports again.

Randomness.

Sloppiness.

Harm without threshold.

That was not what he had done.

He had never acted without pattern confirmation.

He had never targeted unpredictably.

The difference mattered.

He returned to his cell and sat on the lower bunk.

The doubt surfaced again.

Not about guilt.

About consequence.

Had his language enabled instability?

Had he destabilized the very system he believed he was protecting?

The question lingered longer than before.

He examined it carefully.

Systems reject correction.

But systems also distort it.

He had intervened where he perceived fracture.

The world reframed intervention as ideology.

That was not his design.

He closed his eyes.

The ocean returned.

Black water stretching beyond visibility.

Steel railing beneath steady hands.

Wind pressing hard.

He had believed himself guardian.

Perhaps he had misjudged scale.

Perhaps he had mistaken irritation for erosion.

Perhaps.

The word floated for a long moment.

Then—

He reframed it.

Correction without discipline becomes chaos.

He had been disciplined.

Others were not.

The flaw was not intervention.

It was articulation.

He had spoken.

He had allowed philosophy to escape precision.

He opened his eyes slowly.

Across the yard, another inmate shouted.

Guards responded immediately.

Instability contained.

Structure restored.

He leaned back against the cinderblock wall.

The system had neutralized him.

But it had not corrected imbalance.

Outside, cruise ships continued sailing.

Guests boarded.

Arguments erupted.

Entitlement spread in small, unnoticed ways.

Correction no longer belonged to him.

That did not mean imbalance ceased.

He folded his hands over his chest.

Calm settled.

Cold.

Chilling.

Resolved.

"I was necessary," he said quietly.

But this time—

The sentence did not end with certainty.

It ended with awareness.

Necessary does not equal right.

Necessary does not equal contained.

Necessary creates consequence.

The ocean continued without him.

And somewhere beyond steel and concrete—

Someone else was watching.

Coming next…

Dead Sea of Etiquette: The Wake of Correction

The call came at 6:12 a.m.

Nic was already awake.

He had developed that habit since the trial—waking before the world had time to surprise him.

"Mr. Stine?" the voice asked.

"Yes."

"This is Special Agent Ramirez. We need you to come in."

Nic didn't ask why.

He already knew the rhythm of that tone.

The federal building felt colder than it had during the investigation.

Less urgent.

More deliberate.

They sat him down in a conference room with no windows.

Ramirez didn't waste time.

"There's been a development."

Nic's pulse didn't spike.

It flattened.

"What kind of development?"

Ramirez slid a folder across the table.

"Defense counsel has filed a motion to suppress key toxicology evidence."

"On what grounds?"

"Chain of custody. Improper storage transfer during maritime jurisdiction handoff."

Nic stared at him.

"That evidence put him away."

"Yes."

"And now?"

Ramirez held his gaze.

"If the judge agrees, the conviction could be overturned."

The words didn't echo.

They sank.

Overturned.

"He's in maximum security," Nic said.

"For now."

Two weeks later, Nic sat across from Nick Smythe for the first time since sentencing.

Not in a courtroom.

Not in chaos.

In a controlled federal interview room.

Nick wore prison gray.

He looked… rested.

"Did you miss me?" Nick asked lightly.

Nic didn't react.

"You requested this meeting," he said.

Nick smiled faintly.

"I didn't. You did."

Ramirez stood behind the glass.

Watching both of them.

Nick leaned forward slightly.

"You're being questioned now," he said quietly.

"About what?"

"About influence."

Nic's jaw tightened.

"Copycat incidents," Nick continued. "Statements made publicly. Interviews declined. Interviews given. Patterns matter."

The phrase hung there again.

"You think this is my fault?" Nic asked.

"I think," Nick replied calmly, "that once you create a narrative, you don't control who carries it."

Nic studied him.

"You're not getting out."

Nick's expression didn't change.

"Technicalities exist for a reason."

"You exploited access."

"I operated within skill."

"People died."

Nick's eyes sharpened slightly—but not with anger.

"With imbalance," he corrected.

Silence thickened the room.

Nic leaned forward.

"If you walk out of here—"

Nick tilted his head slightly.

"When."

The word was soft.

Confident.

"You think you're necessary," Nic said.

Nick's voice lowered.

"No."

A pause.

"I think the system is predictable."

Outside the room, Ramirez shifted his weight.

He'd seen this look before.

Men who weren't afraid of prison.

Men who were patient.

That night, Nic stood in his driveway staring at the dark.

Beth stepped beside him.

"What did he say?"

Nic didn't look at her.

"He said the system is predictable."

"And?"

Nic exhaled slowly.

"He's not done."

Inside a federal holding facility three states away, Nick lay awake.

Hands folded over his chest.

Calm.

Chain of custody errors are procedural.

Procedural errors create opportunity.

Opportunity restores balance.

He closed his eyes.

Some systems require correction from within.

Others—

From outside.

From Book 2 in the “Dead Sea of Etiquette” series: Dead Sea of Etiquette The Wake of Correction “Because conviction isn’t containment.”

www.ingramcontent.com/pod-product-compliance
Lightning Source LLC
LaVergne TN
LVHW090512110826
845146LV00003B/829

* 9 7 9 8 9 9 5 0 1 1 7 0 5 *